The (Short) Story of My Life

DISCARD

The (Short) Story

of My Life

Jennifer B. Jones

Walker & Company
New York

Especially for my husband, Morgan, whose love and support
enable me to live my dream, and for our children,
Joshua and Aubrey, whose growing-up years provided me
with so many short stories. —J. B. J.

Special thanks to Vicki Berger Erwin for the
"cup of coffee" and so much more.

Copyright © 2004 by Jennifer B. Jones

First published in the United States of America in 2004
by Walker Publishing Company, Inc.

Published simultaneously in Canada by
Fitzhenry and Whiteside, Markham, Ontario L3R 4T8

For information about permission to reproduce selections from this
book, write to Permissions, Walker & Company, 104 Fifth Avenue,
New York, New York 10011

Library of Congress Cataloging-in-Publication Data
Jones, Jennifer B.
The (short) story of my life / Jennifer B. Jones.
p.   cm.
Summary: With both the help and hindrance of family, his best
friend, and the school bully, sixth-grader Michael Jordan copes with
romance and the fact that he is, as usual, the shortest one in his class.
ISBN 0-8027-8905-6
[1. Size—Fiction.   2. Self-perception—Fiction.   3. Schools—
Fiction.   4. Interpersonal relations—Fiction.]   I. Title.
PZ7.J7203Sh   2004
[Fic]—dc22   2003061300

Book design by Jennifer Ann Daddio

Visit Walker & Company's Web site at
www.walkeryoungreaders.com

Printed in the United States of America

2 4 6 8 10 9 7 5 3 1

The (Short) Story of My Life

(1)

Standing Tall

I looked forward to it and dreaded it all summer long. The Labor Day Fair is a big deal in our town. It's the best part of summer, but also the end of it. Labor Day, then the last day of vacation, then back to school. The same every year. Except this year I'd be in the middle school, in the sixth grade. The sixth-graders would be the little kids again. With me the littlest of all.

Everybody in town, and I mean everybody, goes to the ball flats for Labor Day. There are all kinds of carnival rides, games, competitions, and food. And a huge fireworks display to end the day. And summer.

Big booms and bright white, green, blue, and red lighting up the sky, blasting summer to bits. I always go home feeling like I've been to a funeral for summer vacation. Mom and Dad always act like their vacation is just beginning.

My best friend, Ben, and I had each bought a string of tickets for rides at this year's fair.

"Ready, Mike?"

"I don't know," I said. "Let's go on the Tilt-a-Whirl first."

It's not that I didn't *want* to head right for the roller coaster, lock myself into the molded plastic seat, and scream myself silly for the three-minute thrill of a lifetime. I was afraid. Not of the ride, but of not being *allowed* to ride. I'll never forget waiting in line last year, hopping from one foot to the other, handing the carny man my ticket, and then being turned away because I wasn't tall enough to ride without an adult. The humiliation. The *injustice*. The humiliating injustice! I didn't know if I was tall enough this year either, and I wasn't sure if I could handle finding out.

Here's one of the reasons why Ben is my best friend. When I didn't measure up last year, Ben could have handed me his cotton candy and bag of goldfish—the living, breathing, swim-around-afishbowl kind—and enjoyed the coaster without me. But he didn't. Instead, Ben said, "Who wants to ride on this pathetic piece of junk anyway? Let's check out the bumper cars." That's a real friend.

So this year, my real friend and I headed with our arm's length of tickets to the Tilt-a-Whirl line. Dad and my sister, Emma, were just coming off the exit ramp from the ride.

Em came running toward me, her ponytail flopping, *her* newly won goldfish sloshing from one side of the little plastic bag to the other. "Mikey, have you been on the roller coaster yet? That's where Dad and I are going next."

"You boys want to come along?" Dad asked. He was carrying a water bottle, Em's jacket, and a Mylar balloon in the shape of a dog.

"Naw, we have plans," I said, even though I knew it would just kill me if Emma bragged about riding the coaster and I hadn't been allowed to go on.

Dad nodded. "That's what I figured. See you at five then."

"I know. In the food tent for the chicken barbeque." Mom worked in the food tent every year, and we met her there for supper. Dad was always stuck with Emma until then.

Emma pushed the plastic bag toward my face. "Did you see my fish? I named him David."

"You can't do that!" I protested. "That's *my* fish's name."

"Can too," she said. "Lots of people have the same name, like you and Dad. I'll just call my fish *Little David*."

She grinned, then swirled off with Dad, also known as Big Mike. Little David must have felt like he'd been caught in a whirlpool.

"*That,*" I said, pointing at Emma's back, "is the only reason I'm glad summer is ending."

"And this year we get to leave her behind at the elementary school." Ben and I gave each other a high five. "Her fish probably won't live long," he went on. "I don't know anyone who's had a Labor Day fish as long as you've had David. How old is he now?"

"Three years. And he keeps growing and growing." I kicked a pebble with my sneaker. "He'll probably be able to ride the roller coaster before I can."

Ben snorted and slapped me on the back. Ben usually thinks I'm pretty funny.

We ran into other friends now and then all afternoon, but mostly we just hung out together. We

Tilt-a-Whirled, bumper-carred, gobbled up candied apples, slid down the giant slide on burlap sacks, devoured fried dough, checked out the crazy house, and wolfed down cotton candy. We also won three goldfish between us by throwing Ping-Pong balls into fishbowls, and then we gave the poor fish to a little kid who was crying. We stared at the older girls hanging on to older guys my brother Noah's age, and we rode the rest of the rides till we were down to our last ticket each. It was almost five o'clock.

"I guess this is the moment of truth," I said, staring at the one remaining ticket in my hand. "Will this get me on the roller coaster or the merry-go-round?"

"Do you want me to ask the guy how tall you have to be to ride without an adult?" Ben pointed toward the man operating the roller coaster.

"Naw. I can do this," I said with more confidence than I felt.

We waited in line between an older boy with his girlfriend and two girls we didn't know but recognized from our grade. I couldn't care less about the older kids—they were too busy locking lips to notice me anyway—but those girls behind us . . . Last year's humiliation would be nothing compared to what I'd feel if I couldn't ride this year.

The roller-coaster operator took Ben's ticket and nodded for him to go ahead. Then the man looked at me and shook his head. "I don't think so, kid. Better come back with your old lady."

"No, *I* don't think so! I'm older than *him*." I pointed at Ben, who was waiting a couple feet away, mouth hanging open. "I'm older than half the overgrown kids in this line. I'm *short*, okay? Are you going to discriminate against me because of that, or are you going to take this ticket?" I waved it in front of his face.

The man looked surprised for a second, then angry for about two, then his face broke into a grin. Probably because I looked so funny all puffed up with anger. Like a little wet hen.

"How old *are* you, kid?"

"Eleven. And a half!"

"Shoot, my nine-year-old's bigger than you." The man laughed, showing tobacco-stained teeth. "Give me that ticket."

I handed it over and waited for him to tear it in half and boot my fanny all the way to the food tent.

"Get moving before I change my mind." He gave me a little shove toward the green giant that had grown out of the ground overnight, like Jack's beanstalk.

Ben and I started hollering before the coaster got in motion.

(2)

It's the Little Things

On the last day of school in June, the entire fifth grade had walked across our school grounds from the elementary building to the middle-school building. We did this to meet the teachers we'd have for sixth grade when school started again in September.

Mrs. Preston, my sixth-grade homeroom teacher, seemed nice, but all the kids and teachers are on their best behavior on moving-up day, so it was hard to tell.

She explained some things about sixth grade and told us the names of the other teachers on our team.

Told us how we'd be with them for some of our subjects but would be with her for English Language Arts.

Then she handed each of us a notebook. They looked like regular notebooks to me, but she told us that they would be our sixth-grade journals and that we would be writing a page in them every week. She would be reading those pages, every week, and writing something back to us.

On an ordinary school day, this news would have made many of us groan. But like I said, we were on our best behavior. And in less than two hours we would be on summer vacation. Sixth grade seemed years away. No point in worrying about it now.

Then she dropped a bomb. She told us that our first page was due *before* the end of summer vacation!

"That's not fair!" someone I didn't know said. "I'm going to my grandparents' cottage in Canada for the summer."

"Wonderful!" Mrs. Preston clapped her hands together. "Take your journal with you and write about your trip."

Mrs. Preston beamed at us. "That's my advice to all of you who are traveling this summer. Are you flying or driving? Have you ever flown before? Does it frighten or excite you? Are you visiting someone? Why? Who's going with you? What new thing are you doing or trying?" Mrs. Preston paused for a moment. Probably to catch her breath. Maybe to think up more questions for us to answer.

"But I'm not going anywhere," Colby from my fifth-grade class said. "I don't do anything in the summer."

"Then tell me about doing nothing! Or about your pets. Or your friends. Or your favorite video game. Or playing ball or getting sunburned. Or what you had for supper. Or what makes you happy, sad, *angry*. Or what you think sixth grade will be like!" Another breath-catching pause. "I'm sure you get the idea."

Shannon was trying to write down everything that Mrs. Preston was saying. "Please"—our new teacher took a step toward Shannon's desk—"don't try to take notes. Just tell me about *you*, your family, your life, your dreams. You all have so many stories to tell me," she finished.

Shannon looked up from her notebook. "What if we want to write more than a page?"

"Are you crazy?" I blurted out. Everyone but Shannon laughed. Even Mrs. Preston.

"You may write as much as you wish. One page is the minimum. Neat handwriting and no double-spacing."

Philip raised his hand. "You said we had to write our first page before school starts. How are we supposed to get it to you?"

"I was about to tell you that. The main office is open all summer long, so you may drop your journals off with the secretary. Her name is Ms. Wilson. I'll pick them up from her when I come in to prepare our classroom."

Just then an announcement came over the PA system that it was time for us to walk back to our classrooms in the elementary school and gather our things to go home!

"Well, that's it for today, then," Mrs. Preston said. "Have a wonderful summer. Don't forget your journals. I'll see you in September!"

(3)

Monkey in the Middle

I tried to put that journal out of my mind as summer trickled along. I filled my time with swimming, skateboarding, playing soccer on a summer team, ignoring Emma, and annoying Noah. But long summer days can be boring sometimes. On those days my mind worked too much, and I'd worry about the journal. It hung over my head like a storm cloud that hadn't opened up yet but threatened to at any minute.

Emma and I aren't allowed to stay home alone. On weekdays when Noah won't be home and we have nowhere else to go, we have to go with Mom to

Fit and Trim, the fitness center she owns. One morning when we were there, Mom sent us next door to the post office to buy stamps. Mom had given the money to me, but Emma insisted on telling the clerk what we needed, so we stood side by side at the counter. The clerk handed the requested sheet of stamps to Em, and I handed over the money. "There's teamwork," he said. "Are you two twins?"

"No!" I said.

"Well, you sure look like twins," he went on. "Which one of you is older?"

"I am!" Emma and I said in unison. I glared at her, and she giggled.

"No, you're not. I am!" we said at the same time again.

"I get it," the clerk said. "This is some kind of twin trick you play on people."

Em giggled all the way back to Mom's business.

"You are *not* funny," I said to Emma as I handed Mom the change.

"What's the matter?" Mom asked, which is code for "I'm at work. Behave yourselves."

"Mikey is having a *little* problem," Emma explained. She wouldn't stop giggling. When do girls outgrow that?

I would have hopped on one of the empty exercise bikes to work away my frustrations, but I couldn't reach the pedals unless I adjusted the seat. Fat chance I'd do that with Emma around. So instead I went into Mom's office.

"Hey, Mikey," Emma called behind me, "I just thought of something. Most people come here to get *smaller.* And then there's *you.*" She started giggling again.

I ignored Emma and dumped out my backpack on Mom's desk. My GameBoy and headset tumbled out. So did my soccer jersey, some candy wrappers, and the journal. What the heck.

I opened it up and stared at the first page. The only thing on the whiteness of it was thin blue lines. The kind you're supposed to write between. I counted them up. There were twenty-three of them. I had to fill a whole page every week. That was twenty-three lines of writing. Good grief. I put the date at the top of the first page and began to write.

July 21

I might as well tell you right up front. My name is Michael Jordan. The third. I am not related to the basketball player. I have never even met him. And I am not <u>named</u> after him. I am named after my father who was named after <u>his</u> father, the original Michael Jordan. Maybe the basketball player was named after my grandpa. How do I know? All I know is I'm short. And I hate basketball. I wouldn't play it if you paid me. And why would you pay me? My own sister won't pick me when she plays in our driveway.

Anyway, it doesn't matter to me that I am short. I could care less.

You probably remember me sitting in your class on moving-up day. I was the one who had a hard time seeing over the desk. You will probably decide to put my seat near the board so no one blocks my view.

When I tell people my name for the first time, they almost always laugh. Sometimes they say something stupid like, "<u>The</u> Michael Jordan?" or "Can I have your autograph?" Then they laugh some more. How am I supposed to answer questions like that? I usually don't answer them at all. Questions like that don't deserve answers.

You said we could write about our families.

My mom—Beth—is no giant either, but she's a girl, so her size doesn't matter. She says it never bothered her to be the smallest in her class. She says that good things come in small packages. Try telling that to the guys in the locker room.

Everyone else in my family is average height. They always say things about a person's height not mattering. Not that I care about it one way or another, but really, what do they know?

In addition to my mom, I have a *younger* sister, a dad, and an older brother. Being the middle child in the family, I'm what you could call the monkey in the middle. Or the shrimp in the shrimp sandwich.

Sometimes people want to know why my older brother didn't inherit the name Michael. That's a question I <u>can</u> answer. He was named after my mom's dad, Noah. My sister is Emma Joy after both my grandmas. I guess by the time she was born, my parents had decided they didn't want any more girls, so they better use up both names at once. If I ever have kids, they will <u>not</u> be named after anyone. I will probably invent names to make sure nobody else, dead or alive, has them.

I stopped writing then. I had filled three whole pages in my notebook journal! That was sixty-nine lines of writing. It hadn't taken me very long. And I felt a lot better. I was free for the rest of the summer.

Then I thought of something I should add, so I wrote on the top of page *four:*

> When I said my whole family is average height except my mom, I was talking about my immediate family. Everyone in my mom's family is short. Grandma Joy is practically a midget. Grandpa calls her his little bundle of Joy. I don't think anyone will ever say that about my sister.

That added six more lines!

(4)

Great Expectations

"**D**oes Emma have to walk with Ben and me?" I asked Mom on the first day of school. "It's not fair that Noah leaves ahead of us, and we're stuck with Em."

"The high school starts an hour earlier than your schools. You know that. And yes, you have to walk with her." Mom squirted liquid that looked like lemon pudding into the little dispenser inside the dishwasher door, closed it, and pressed the buttons. The motor clicked on, and water began filling the machine.

"I don't want to walk with them!" Emma complained. "I told Kimmy I'd walk with her."

"Fine," Mom said. "Fine. I just don't want either of you walking alone. Oh, pictures! We have to take your first-day-of-school pictures before you leave." Mom scurried into the dining room and took the digital camera out of the cupboard.

Great. More proof for future years that "Those two *did* look like twins! Same brown hair, same brown eyes. Even the same size." At least we didn't *dress* the same.

"Let's sit on the porch swing," I suggested. "That would be a nice background." I was really thinking that I didn't want to *stand* next to Emma in another picture, but I thought the bit about background was a nice touch.

Mom and Emma agreed. Ben arrived while Mom took the yearly photos, and she made him get in a shot with us—a redhead to break up the monotony of the Jordan family photos. Then Mom kissed Em good-bye. Ben and I grabbed our backpacks and hurried off the porch.

"Have a good day, boys!" Mom smiled and waved. She loved the first day of school. I thought about how happy moms all over the world must be on that day.

"I can't believe summer's over," Ben moaned.

We talked about how awesome the fair had been, and how I'd stood up for myself to the roller-coaster man.

"I think that is a good sign," I said. "I think this is going to be a big year for me."

When we arrived on campus, I noticed the younger kids, including Emma and Kimmy, heading toward the elementary school. My chest puffed up a little as Ben and I turned down the walkway to the middle school. I felt taller already.

"Hey, kid," I heard from behind. I turned and saw a huge boy gaining on me.

"Yeah, you," he said. "You're in the wrong place. The elementary school is over there." He pointed to it.

"I'm in sixth grade," I told him, feeling myself sink into my sneakers.

"Wow. Are you a genius or something?"

"Yeah, he's something." Ben put his arm around my shoulders to keep me moving into the building. But the big kid noticed a group of his friends and lost interest in us.

"Did you get a good look at him? He looks older than Noah. I think he had whiskers."

Ben shrugged. "Maybe he was left back."

"A few times," I said, and we laughed.

"He looks old enough to drive!" Ben added.

As we walked to our classroom I noticed that everybody had grown a lot over the summer. Especially the girls. They looked different from how they had in fifth grade. My dream about having a big year seemed to be fading already.

"Hello, Mike," Mrs. Preston said as I entered the room. At first I thought that she remembered who I was because of my size, but she greeted Ben, Philip, Colby, and everyone else who came in by name. This teacher was full of surprises. I wondered if I should be nervous about that.

It took a while that day for desks and lockers and books to be assigned to everyone. And to tour the building. And to meet all the teachers on our team and find out how they planned to run the show. Ben and I ended up in all the same classes, including the two we had with Mrs. Preston—ELA (English Language Arts) and math.

After lunch, Mrs. Preston returned our notebook journals and said that because it was a short week, she'd give us time that afternoon to begin our next entry.

In my notebook she had written in thin, swirly

cursive, "I'm very impressed with your three pages plus six lines of writing! I enjoyed reading about your family. Perhaps sometime you would like to tell me about a sport you *do* enjoy!"

That's it? I thought. Only four lines? But then I remembered that we have twenty-two kids in our class. If she wrote four lines for everyone, that would be a lot of writing every week!

I dated the top of the next clean page. Then wrote in my best handwriting:

I like soccer. I play on a summer team, and I am a forward. I wish there was a fall school team for sixth-graders in our town like there is for high school. I know I will make the team when I'm old enough to play. I can't wait to be one of the Titans! Even though I am short, I am quick and wiry. In one of our games this summer, I scored a hat trick. That means I made three goals. I also had two assists in that game. That means that I helped other people score goals two times. That was my best game ever. While I was running hard toward the goal I heard my coach yell, "Yeah, Mikey. Look at those little legs go!" I like it when people are amazed at my speed. What I don't like are "one-size-fits-all"

jerseys. Mine fit me all right—like a dress. When I
wore it to our first game, a smart-mouthed kid on
the other team asked me if I had any high heels to
go with it. My sister, Emma, laughed and laughed
at that one. Later, when she had her friend Kimmy
over, she said to me, "Mikey, can I borrow your
dress?" Ha ha ha.

I had spilled a few lines onto the next page, so I
quit. I could have told Mrs. Preston about my
older brother, Noah, who *does* like basketball and
probably would be on the JV—that means junior
varsity—team this winter. Noah likes most sports.
He was playing JV soccer now and would probably
run track in the spring, even though he isn't super-
fast like me. Maybe I'd tell her that stuff another
time, but I had to be careful about not going over
one page right now. I didn't want Mrs. Preston to
expect too much of me, especially at the beginning
of the year.

(5)

Short but Sweet

On Friday morning Ben and I went to the school store before morning announcements to buy the assignment books Mrs. Preston wanted us to have. The school store is really a counter full of school supplies set up in our library every morning. It's run by eighth-graders.

"What kind of person would want to get here early every day to *work* before *school?*" Ben shook his head.

"That kind," I said, nodding toward a pretty girl with blond hair. She was opening a box of square pink erasers.

Ben and I found the assignment books we needed. The pretty girl took our money.

"Weren't you at the JV soccer game yesterday?" she said to me.

"Yeah. My brother is on the team. Noah Jordan, number five."

"That's what I thought," she said. "My brother's the goalie."

I nodded. "He's good."

The blond girl smiled. "So's your brother."

"Thanks. Well, bye." I didn't know what else to say, and other kids were waiting to pay for stuff.

"I'll look for you at the games. Go Titans!" The blond girl smiled and waved.

Once Ben and I were alone in the hall, I blurted it out. "I think I'm in love."

"With who?" He jumped up, trying to touch the bottom of the doorway casing at the entrance to our wing of the building.

"I don't know her name. That blond girl back there."

Ben turned around to look behind us.

"No. Back there in the library," I said.

"You're kidding, right?" Ben snorted.

"Why would I be kidding about something this serious?"

"For one thing, you just met her, you don't even know her name, and in case you don't already know this . . . she's two years older, and a lot taller, than you."

"That hurts," I said. "That's a very low blow."

"Sorry, man." He slugged my arm. "I just think I need to be honest. You have a better chance of . . . of . . . making the NBA than scoring with an eighth-grader."

"I guess. But I can dream, can't I?"

"You crack me up," Ben said. "You really do." He jumped up and slapped the casing above the doorway to our room.

D ad brought pizza home that night. He usually picks up something for our supper after work on Fridays. Usually he and Mom eat with us. Sometimes they go out by themselves. This was a usual Friday night.

"So, how'd the first week back at school go for everyone?" Dad asked as we filled our plates with pizza and fruit salad.

"I love Mr. Morris," Emma said. "He is funny, and he used to work in a zoo. We are going to have our own animal fair in the spring. I think I'll need to get a guinea pig or a hamster or something so I'll have an animal to put in the fair."

"We'll see," Mom said, but her face looked like Emma wouldn't be getting a rodent of any kind any time soon.

"Take Ben's dog," I suggested.

"*That's* where you got your fleas from," Noah said, pointing at me.

"You're so funny I forgot to laugh," I told him.

"We can't borrow animals unless their owners come too," Emma told me in her I-know-more-about-it-than-you-do voice.

"Then take Little David. If he's still alive."

"I bet he'll be alive a lot longer than *your* smelly old fish!"

Dad cleared his throat. "What do you think of the middle school?" he asked me.

"It's okay. We don't get treated like *little* kids." I smirked at Emma. "Mrs. Preston returned our journals and gave us time to write in them."

"I hope I get her," Emma said, "unless Mr. Morris moves up to sixth grade. I'd keep him forever."

"You say that about your teachers every year," I reminded her.

"So."

"So, Noah," Dad changed the subject again, "any news about school? Or soccer?"

Noah had just jammed half a slice of veggie-with-extra-cheese pizza into his mouth. Mom filled our water glasses—she's big on drinking water—while we waited for his answer.

"I have to buy a biology Regents review book. We're selling fruit and cookie dough to raise money for new soccer uniforms. And I have to pay for a year-book when I order it next Tuesday."

Dad shook his head. "I'm sorry I asked."

"Who's your goalie?" I blurted.

"Dave O'Rourke," Noah answered. "He's a pretty cool guy. Why?"

I shrugged like it was no big deal. "His sister is in my school. She said she was at the game Thursday afternoon."

Noah washed down his slice of pizza with a big gulp of water and grabbed another slice. "Yeah, I saw her with him afterward. I think he called her Macy."

"Whatever." I tried to sound bored, but hearing

her name made my heart pound. My face must have turned red.

"Mikey has a girlfriend!" Emma squealed.

"Do not! She's in eighth grade, dork."

"No name-calling, Michael," Mom said. "Emma, chill."

Dad put his hand on Mom's arm. "Where would you like to go next Friday night, Beth?"

"I like Chinese food," Mom said. "How about China?"

(6)

What Are
Big Brothers For?

It was raining Monday morning, so Mom dropped us kids off at school on her way to work. I wasn't able to talk to Ben till lunchtime. He banged his lunch tray against mine and sat beside me at the crowded cafeteria table.

"Her name is Macy," I told him.

"Whose name?" Ben peeled the wrapper off his ice-cream sandwich and began to eat it.

"You know, the girl at the school store. The goalie's sister. Macy O'Rourke." I opened up the sandwich Mom had packed in my nutritious lunch, removed the lettuce and tomato, and covered the sliced turkey with potato chips I had bought in the lunch line.

"Are you still thinking about her?" Ben shook his head. "You really need to give it a rest."

I ignored his remark. "I think I'll go back and buy one of those little pink erasers. I love those things." I crunched into my sandwich.

"You don't need an eraser. You bought all new supplies before school started."

"You can never have too many erasers," I told him. "Especially with all this journal writing we have to do."

"About that," Ben said, frowning. "Why do we have to do it?"

"I don't know." I shrugged. "I think she wants us to practice writing. Maybe she's nosy." I popped a grape into my mouth.

"What did she write in yours this time?" Ben had finished his ice cream and had moved on to a bag of corn chips.

I snorted. "Something about how little sisters can be annoying at times but can be a lot of fun too. She thought I might like to tell her about something Emma and I enjoy doing together. Right. How about watching the same TV show—me in the TV room, and Em in Mom and Dad's bedroom."

"Emma's not that bad. For a little sister," Ben said. He breathed on his spoon and hung it off his nose.

"That's just it," I said. "She wasn't bad when she *was* my little sister. But when she got as big as me, she got too bigheaded and bossy."

Ben laughed, and the spoon fell off his nose.

We didn't have time for writing that day. But I was still thinking about Mrs. Preston's comments when I met up with Emma at Fit and Trim after school.

"Hey, Em, remember how we used to slide down the laundry chute?"

Emma laughed. "That was fun. Why did Mom have to make us stop?"

I shrugged. "I guess she was afraid we'd get hurt coming down."

"But we always made sure there was a big pile of laundry below us to land on," Emma said.

"Maybe she thought we'd get stuck inside it." As soon as I said that, I thought Em would make a joke about how even though *she* might have grown big enough to get stuck, *I* sure hadn't. But Emma was busy remembering.

"I was afraid to go down the first time. You went

ahead of me and told me it was easy, like going down a slide."

"The first time *I* went down was to rescue you," I said, as if she'd never heard the story before. "You were three years old and had locked yourself in the downstairs bathroom. Mom didn't have a key, and the only thing she could think to do was send me down the chute to unlock the door from the inside. She didn't want me to do it, but *she* couldn't fit down the chute, and she didn't know what else to do."

"I got into everything." Emma was very proud of how mischievous she had been as a toddler. She had also adored me back then. And I had loved being her big brother.

"Remember how I used to call you Almond Joy?" I asked her.

Emma laughed. "Because I was such a nut."

I laughed too, then looked around to make sure Mom wasn't nearby. "Should we go down the chute again sometime? When Mom's not home?"

"Yes!" Emma said. Her ponytail bobbed up and down as she nodded her head.

We slapped our hands together in a high five, and I felt like we were partners in crime again.

The next day I wrote about Emma and me and

our laundry chute. I explained how it goes from our upstairs bathroom to the downstairs bathroom below, where the washer and dryer are. When we are upstairs, all we have to do is lift the lid to a box that looks like a hamper and throw our clothes in. They slide down a big plastic tube and land in a bin below. I told about rescuing Emma after she'd locked herself in the downstairs bathroom, and how, later on, Em and I pretended we were at the park and slid down ourselves. And how Mom had stopped us. I don't know why she thought it was any different from a real slide.

When I finished, I felt like I had written a story. I decided to give it a title. In the margin at the top of the page I wrote "Chute Me." I could hardly wait for Mrs. Preston to read it. I'd never had the best grades in English Language Arts, but I thought they would be different this year. And thanks to Macy's school job, I'd be sure to stay stocked up on all the writing supplies I'd need.

(7)

Having a Little Trouble

The next day I discovered that Macy O'Rourke does not work in the school store on Wednesdays. I took my time looking everything over, hoping she'd come in. I waited as long as I could, then bought the pink eraser I didn't even need.

I was afraid people would start to wonder what I was up to if I went to the library every single morning, so Ben scoped things out for me on Thursday. I gave him my ice-cream money so he could buy something. He came back to our classroom shaking his head. "Maybe she only works on Fridays."

"I should have checked on Monday and Tuesday,"

I said, disgusted with myself. "Wait a minute. This is Thursday! Maybe she'll be at the soccer game after school."

"Maybe, but you're coming to my house, remember?"

"I don't know, Ben. I forgot about the game. Why don't you come with me?"

"I guess I'll have to. Someone has to protect you from yourself."

Before Ben and I could go to the game, we had to walk to Ben's house to tell his mom our change in plans. Then Ben decided to take his basset hound, Homer, with us. Homer sniffed every tree and telephone pole along the way. He was also interested in the new drainage pipes that the Department of Public Works was putting in along the roadway. Homer is a slow and curious dog.

The game had started by the time we showed up. Mom and Emma were already there. I noticed that Macy was too, but I didn't think she'd seen us arrive. Would she be able to tell that I'd hoped to see her there?

"Homer!" Emma squealed, racing toward us.

Homer gave a husky hound bark of recognition and picked up speed, jerking Ben forward.

Em knelt to hug the wiggling dog. "Can I take him over there?" Emma pointed to where some other kids were playing, a short distance away but in sight of the parents who were watching the game.

"As long as you keep him off the soccer field," Ben said, handing Em Homer's leash. "He has a mind of his own," Ben called after them.

"So does she," I said. "I wouldn't worry about either one of them."

We noticed Mom's and Emma's empty lawn chairs. Mom always brings them but paces up and down the sidelines instead of sitting. Later in the season the chairs would be holding blankets and a thermos of hot cocoa.

We tracked Mom down close to our goal. "What's the score?" I asked her.

"One to nothing, our favor," Mom said without taking her eyes off the game. "But the other team is aggressive. They're taking lots of shots and putting our goalie to the test." As she finished speaking, a ball sailed toward the top right corner of the goal. Dave O'Rourke leaped up high and sideways and blocked it from going in.

Our fans started to shout, "We are the Titans, the mighty mighty Titans!"

"That was close," I said.

Mom shook her head. "I don't know how long he can keep that up." Then her voice changed to a shout as my brother took possession of the ball. "Go, Noah, go!" Mom headed up the sidelines, chasing the action. She looked like a little bitty coach, running along in a navy blue tracksuit.

An opposing player tripped Noah. The referee blew his whistle and quickly set up a foul shot.

I felt a change in the air, almost like the static electricity that sometimes comes off socks that have been in the dryer, and turned to see Macy standing beside me.

"Exciting, isn't it?" she breathed.

I looked up at her and gulped. "What?"

"The game, silly. Isn't it exciting?"

"Oh, yes! Very. I, we, my friend Ben and I"—I nudged him—"got here just in time to see your brother's last save. He's great."

"Yeah, great," Ben repeated. He was staring at Macy and had a goofy grin on his face.

"I know he's good," she said, "but I don't come just to watch him. I come to see other people." She smiled so wide that her cheeks scrunched up her eyes. I'd never seen anything so beautiful in my life.

Ben jabbed me in the ribs, and I closed my mouth.

"Me too," I said weakly, but the action was directly in front of us again, and Macy was watching the game.

The horn sounded to end the first half of the game. The score was still one to nothing. The players headed for their benches on opposite sides of the field.

"Well, I guess I'll go back and sit with my family." Macy was looking in that direction. "I just wanted to say hi."

"Hi," Ben said, grinning like a village idiot. I scowled at him.

"Bye," I said to Macy. We watched her walk back to where her parents were sitting. She passed by the Titans' bench very slowly, probably because she wanted to say something to her brother, but he was too busy listening to the coach to notice.

"You should have talked to her more," Ben complained. "She might have stayed if you'd talked to her!"

"What was I supposed to say?"

"I don't know. But I think she likes you, man."

Ben grinned and shook his head. "I don't get it. Why you?"

"Why *not* me?" I asked. "I'm young, I know. And short. But I'm also very good-looking. And I'm funny. She said so herself."

"She called you *silly*. That's a little different than funny. You better figure out how to talk to her soon, or she's going to lose interest in you. Girls are like that. So I've heard."

I'm usually pretty interested in soccer games, but I couldn't stop thinking about Macy. I was glad when we scored another goal because it gave me an excuse to whoop and holler without making people wonder why I was so happy. Every little while I'd look up in the stands to see what Macy was doing, and I'd wish the game would last forever.

Dad hadn't been able to make it to the game, so Noah filled him in during supper. "Dave was amazing, Dad. He didn't let them score once!"

"I didn't watch the game. I played with Homer," Emma said. "He ran right through a big pipe for me. I pretended we were at a dog show."

"What big pipe was that?" Dad asked.

"The village is putting in new drainage pipes under some driveways along Canal Street," Mom said. "They left a few of them on the ball flats. I guess so they're not in people's yards."

"Noah had an assist, Dad," I said.

"Congratulations." Dad reached across the table to give Noah a high five. "Well done."

Noah looked happy. "I'm going to O'Rourke's after practice tomorrow. If that's okay."

That's when the bite of chicken I was swallowing stopped going down and stuck in my throat.

"What about supper?" Mom asked Noah as she scooped rice pilaf onto her plate.

"I'm eating there. I've been invited." Noah loaded his fork with tossed salad.

I clutched my throat with both of my hands.

"That's all right, then," Mom said.

Emma noticed that something was wrong with me. "I think Michael is choking!"

Mom jumped out of her seat, crashing it to the floor, and yanked me out of mine. She wrapped her arms around me from behind and squeezed me in the Heimlich maneuver. The chicken chunk flew out of my mouth and landed on the table.

"Gross!" Emma said, wrinkling her nose.

"*I'm* done eating." Noah pushed his plate away.

"What happened, Michael? Are you all right?" Mom hovered over me as I sat back down.

I nodded my head.

"Have some water." Mom handed me my glass, and I took a shaky sip.

"Is he okay?" Dad asked, hands ready on the table in case he needed to stand.

"I'm fine," I said.

"Wish I could say the same," Noah said. "Way to go, Mike."

"Noah!" Mom said, then returned her attention to me. "Michael," she scolded, "you need to slow down and chew your food."

I nodded again. But nobody felt like chewing and swallowing anything more that night.

(8)

I Could Use a Little Help

When I could talk and swallow better later that evening, I called Ben. "Hey," I said, "how can you make chicken fly after it's cooked?"

"Is this one of your stupid jokes?"

"No, I'm serious!"

"I don't know," he said. "Put it on an airplane?"

"Very funny, but no." I told him about Mom giving me the Heimlich and how the chicken had flown out of my mouth and ruined everyone's dinner.

"Cool!" he said. "What made you choke?"

Then I told him what Noah had said about going to O'Rourke's on Friday night.

"To see *Macy*?" he asked.

"No, you numbskull. He's friends with Dave, remember? Even though he surprised me at first, I started thinking that if Dave and Noah become really good friends, maybe he'll take me over there sometime so I can hang out with Macy while he's with Dave."

"Or, if you start talking to Macy more, maybe *she'll* ask you to come over."

I was doodling on the chalkboard by the phone. Wavy lines that looked like cursive *M*'s, and circles. Or the letter *O*. "I think I need a new ruler. I'll pick one up at the school store tomorrow morning."

"If you keep this up, you'll be able to open your own store by the end of the year."

"Maybe Macy and I will go into business together." I laughed. Yes, I just might be able to use Noah's friendship with Dave to my advantage.

The next morning I went to the library. Macy came right over to me. I explained why I was there.

"Do you want a wooden ruler or a plastic one?" She held up one of each. "The wooden one is sturdier, but the plastic one has holes so you can put it in a three-ring binder." I was inspecting them closely when one of the other eighth-grade store workers rudely interrupted.

"Who's the little kid, Macy? One of your students? Or a visitor from the elementary school, perhaps?"

"He happens to be a friend, Wes. Though it's none of your business." Wes just stood there grinning. "Did you need something?" Macy asked him.

Wes just winked, then carried a box of assorted portfolios to the other end of the counter.

Macy rolled her eyes. "Wes Powers. What a creep," she said to me in a low voice. "I'm thinking about asking if I can work a different day so I'm not here with him every Friday."

"What did he mean when he asked if I was one of your students?" I whispered back.

"I'm a peer tutor. I help kids with math during activity period on Wednesdays. I tried to help him once, but he's not really interested in math, if you know what I mean. Creep." She rolled her eyes again.

"I could use some math help," I blurted.

"Really?"

"Yeah," I said. "Do I have to sign up or something?"

"You have to have your teacher's permission to come to Mr. Potter's room at two-thirty. Bring some work you're having trouble with, and someone will help you."

"It wouldn't be you?" I asked. I hoped my voice didn't sound whiny. Like Emma's.

"Whoever is free helps. But I'd do my best to work with you." Now *she* winked.

The last morning bell was ringing, so I had to quickly pay for the plastic ruler and leave. I didn't even have time to find out if she knew Noah would be at her house later that day.

When I told Ben about my conversation with Macy, he was amazed. "*I'm* the one who could use help in math," he said.

"I know. I just kind of blurted it out so I could see her. I'm no better than that creep Wes. I'm supposed to take some work I need help with, but I don't have any."

"Take one of my papers," Ben suggested. He showed me his last homework paper and quiz.

"That's not a bad idea. Maybe you should go for tutoring yourself."

"Spend activity period *studying?* I don't think so!"

Ben shook his head like I'd told one of my stupid jokes.

"You may not have a choice." I handed the papers back to him. "Want to spend the night? You can help me get info out of Noah when he gets home."

(9)

A Perfect Fit

The phone was ringing as Mom, Em, and I were coming into the house from work and school that afternoon. Emma ran to grab it.

"Big Mike or Little Mike?" I heard her ask the caller. "Just a minute." Then she handed the phone to me.

"Let me guess," I said to her. "They want Big Mike."

"Hello?" I said into the receiver. Ben was on the other end of the line. "When Nerd Brain answers the phone," I said to him, "why can't you just ask to speak to her brother, Mike? Would that be so difficult?"

"I heard that!" Nerd Brain hollered.

"Good!" I said to her. "Now we know that you *hear* better than you *smell*."

Nerd Brain stuck out her tongue, then huffed out of the room.

"Emma is going to Kimmy's for supper," I told Ben. "If you want to eat with us, I'll call Dad and let him know what kind of sub sandwich to bring you. Otherwise it will be something on a whole wheat bun."

"Thank you, Mr. and Mrs. Jordan," Ben said when we were excused from the table a short time later.

"Glad to have you, Ben," my dad said, patting Ben on the shoulder.

Mom nodded. "It's always nice when people aren't arguing during supper."

"What do you want to do now?" I asked Ben.

"How about a little laser tag?"

We got the stuff from my bedroom and took it outside.

Ben ran out back, and I squeezed into a space under the front porch and waited. A couple minutes later he peered around the corner of the house. He didn't see me. He was checking for me in the tree, behind the shrub, and *on* the porch, but not under it. He headed in my direction. When he got close enough, I zapped him with my laser.

"You have an unfair advantage," he squawked. "You can hide in places I can't fit into."

I crawled out and brushed the dirt off my jeans. "Don't you think I deserve an advantage because of my size once in a while?"

"You can run faster than me too," he complained.

"Okay," I said, taking off at full speed toward the back of the house, "if it's too small for you, it's off-limits for the game. But I'm not slowing down!"

When we were tired of tag, we went inside to watch a movie and wait for Noah. He didn't get home till almost nine o'clock. He joined us in the TV room.

"Want some of our popcorn?" I held the bowl out to him, hoping he'd stick around and talk.

"Nah." Noah rubbed his belly. "I just had a soda and chips at O'Rourke's."

"What else did you do there?" I asked, hoping I didn't sound too eager.

He shrugged. "Not much. We ate, talked. Watched a movie."

"Was Macy there?" Ben asked without any prompting from me. I guess it was good I hadn't zapped him from any more small places.

"She was." Noah laughed, remembering something. "She thinks you're pretty cute, Mike. *I* think she needs to have her eyes examined."

I laughed, too, because I was so nervous. I thought about how pretty Macy's eyes are when they're all scrunched up. About how pretty she'd be with glasses.

Noah threw a pillow at Ben. "Staying over, Ben Dover?"

"Yup," Ben said. He rolled his eyes and said for the millionth time during our friendship, "You do know that's not my name, don't you?"

Noah laughed again and went up to his room.

(10)

Tall Tale

Grandma and Grandpa Harris, also known as Joy and Noah, came to visit that Sunday. As soon as they walked in the back door, Grandpa boomed, "The little people have arrived! Where is everybody?"

Noah was in his room using his computer, Emma had her nose in some animal book, Mom was folding laundry, and Dad and I were watching TV. But we all raced to the kitchen when we heard Grandpa's voice.

Grandma had a large pocketbook that looked like a suitcase when she was holding it over her arm. She set it down and flung her arms open wide. Emma was the first to reach them. "Goodness, Emma Joy,"

Grandma said, "you are going to be taller than me by the time we come home from Florida next spring! And look at *you*," she said to Noah. "Did you get any of the Harris genes at all?" Noah had to bend over to kiss her.

"Hi, Grandma," I said, moving in for my hug.

"Oh, Mikey, hello dear. You remind me so much of your grandpa when he was a boy."

"Must be fighting the girls off with a stick, eh, Mike?" Grandpa said with a wink.

"What nonsense you talk, old man." Grandma bopped him on the head. "I was the only girl who ever gave you a second look."

"That's because you were the only one who could look at me eye to eye!" Grandpa chuckled at himself. Everybody laughed.

"She wanted to marry a jockey," he continued. "I met the height requirement, but the horses always complained about my weight." Grandpa patted his round belly. Grandma bopped him on the head again.

"My brother was a fine jockey, and I can't even get *him*"—Grandma shook her finger at Grandpa—"*near* a horse." Then, turning to me, she said, "Michael, *you* should be a jockey. It takes a very special person, you know."

"I'll think about it, Grandma," I said, not wanting to disappoint her. But growing up to be a jockey was the furthest thing from my mind.

Now Grandma had a suggestion for my parents. "Why don't you get Michael a horse?"

"Me too!" Emma pranced around the room, her ponytail swishing back and forth.

"I bet the neighbors would love that," Dad said.

Grandpa chuckled and slapped his leg.

"Laugh if you want," Grandma retorted. "I'm just being realistic. Not everyone can be a basketball player like that *other* Jordan boy, you know."

I love my funny little grandparents, but the older I got, the more afraid I became that I was going to grow up, or *not* grow up, just like them. At least now I knew that girls—not just the little ones—could like me. Did like me!

Everybody had lots of news to share. We all stayed around the kitchen table till after dinner. Then Mom and Emma took Gram to show her the changes at Fit and Trim. I helped clear the table, and Dad and Noah started to do the dishes.

"What say we head outside, Mike," Grandpa said to me. "I need to stretch my legs."

"Thanks for getting me out of dishes, Grandpa," I said once we were on the porch.

"Don't mention it." Gramp's eyes twinkled. "Looks like *your* legs could use some stretching too!" We reached the end of the driveway and kept walking up the block.

"Gramp, did you ever get sick of being short?"

"Course I did! In fact, I didn't just get sick of being short, I nearly died of it."

I stopped walking and stared at him.

"That's right," he went on. He motioned for me to keep moving. "It was during a big snowstorm we had last century, back when I was a boy. Biggest storm you ever saw. It started one Saturday morning, and by Sunday evening we had fifty-three inches of the white stuff. Do the math, Mikey. That's over four feet of snow. In a little over twenty-four hours! My mother sent me out to play when the snow was coming down at a rate of over two inches an hour. I started to build a snowman, and by the time I got done, I was so covered with snow that I couldn't move. My mother looked out the window to check on me, and all she saw were *two* snowmen. She had no idea that one of them was me and that I was stuck fast in that pile of snow! My family searched and called all the neighbors. They about decided I'd gotten too close to the road and been scooped up by a snowplow. By the time they found me, I was nearly frozen to death." Grandpa shivered, then went on. "We had three snow days because of that storm. Good thing. I wasn't thawed out till Wednesday night and couldn't hold on to a pencil till Thursday morning."

"Grandpa, you're kidding me, right?"

"What makes you think so?" Grandpa was trying to look serious.

"Because I never heard you talk about it before. The only big storm you've told me about happened the year I was born, and we have pictures of Noah out on the shoveled sidewalk with Dad. The snowbanks on either side are over Dad's head."

"In a storm like that, Mike, everybody is small." Grandpa winked at me.

"That's a great story, Gramp. Maybe I'll write it in my school journal."

"You do that," he said, squeezing my shoulder with his thick, stubby fingers. "It'll give your teacher a good laugh." Grandpa buttoned his sweater. "I'm glad I wore this. The sun feels good, but there's a nip in the air."

I realized then that the leaves were changing. "I guess summer's really over."

"All good things come to an end. Speaking of which, we better head back to the house. If your Grandma is back, she'll be itching to get on the road."

"Do you have to leave tonight?"

"'Fraid so. But we'll get together again before we head south."

"When will that be?"

"Before the snow flies. Don't dare take a chance on getting lost in another snowdrift. Or worse yet, losing my little bundle of Joy!"

We both laughed. "Gramp, I wish I'd inherited your sense of humor."

"You do fine. You just have to let the funny grow, son. Especially when nothing else will." He ruffled my hair with his fat fingers.

Once we were all back at the house, Mom was able to talk Grandma and Grandpa into waiting till morning to go home.

I didn't have another chance to talk to Grandpa

alone, but when I went to bed that night, I thought a lot about the things he'd said to me. His story had been funny, but the thing I liked best was thinking about how something really big, like a huge snowstorm, evens everybody up. I'd have to remember that.

One Little Thing After Another

Since Grandma and Grandpa were heading home about the time Emma and I needed to leave for school, they insisted on dropping us off. "It's a chilly morning," Grandma said, hugging herself.

"I walk with Ben," I told them. "He'll be here any minute."

"He can come too," Grandma said.

"What about Kimmy?" Emma asked.

"The more the merrier," Gramp said. "I've always wondered what it would be like to drive a school bus."

So we loaded up, Ben and me in the backseat of

their van and the girls in the middle because they'd be getting out first. Grandpa told funny stories all the way to school.

"See you in a few weeks," Gram said as Ben and I climbed out in front of our building.

"Stay out of deep snow!" Grandpa hollered out his window.

"Now I know where you get it from." Ben jabbed my arm.

"What, my size?"

"No, your corny jokes. You're just like him."

"Thank you," I said, pulling myself up straighter. "I take that as a compliment."

We were a little early, so I decided to speak to Mrs. Preston about the math tutoring. Ben decided to hide in the boys' room for a few minutes so Mrs. Preston wouldn't get any ideas about sending him for tutoring too.

"You're doing just fine in math," she told me.

"So far," I admitted, "but it's starting to seem pretty hard. And I don't want to get lost this early in the year."

"I usually wait a few weeks so children have a chance to settle in before I recommend tutoring, but if you think it's necessary, I'm happy to send you. Perhaps your friend Ben will join you."

"I think he just needs time to settle," I said quickly. "He gets pretty flighty over summer vacation."

Mrs. Preston laughed. "You're going to do very well this year, Michael. You have a good work ethic."

I wasn't too sure about my work ethic, mostly because I didn't know what it meant. But I did feel like a pretty good friend. Ben might end up in tutoring, but it would be his doing, not mine. I'd saved his activity periods for now.

When Mrs. Preston handed back our journals during ELA, I looked right away to see what she'd written. Beneath my "Chute Me" paragraphs it said, "You did a great job turning a memory into a story! Do you have any more to share with me?"

Do I ever, I thought. I could hardly wait to write Grandpa's tall tale.

By the time we went home that day, the sky was gray, and it had started to rain.

"I wish your grandpa was here to give us a ride now," Ben said, rubbing his hands together.

"And this is just the beginning. We'll be walking through snow in a few more weeks," I said. Leaves hadn't even fallen from the trees yet, but I guess once it snows in your brain, it takes a while to melt away.

"You know what that means?" Ben's face lit up.

"Snow days!" we sang together.

It was still raining after school the next day. I went to Noah's soccer game anyway. Mom was running up and down the sidelines in her yellow slicker, but I didn't see the lawn chairs. She probably figured there was no sense getting them wet when no one was going to use them.

I'd planned to tell Macy that I'd be showing up for tutoring the next day, but she wasn't there. I hoped she just didn't like getting rained on and not that she was sick or something.

I hate playing soccer in the rain. It's cold, the wet uniform sticks to your skin, the grass is slippery, and once your hair is completely soaked, little rivers of water run off it right into your eyes.

Noah got in a battle for the ball that ended with him on the ground, trampled by someone's soccer cleats. He had to sit out the rest of the game with an ice pack on his shin. And worse than that, a wet ball slipped right through Dave's fingers into the goal, and we lost the game by one point.

The next day dragged on and on. I tried to help it along by entertaining my classmates at lunchtime. I managed to trade the apple Mom had packed in my lunch for Colby's cheese twists and immediately stuck two of them up my nose and announced that I was a walrus. I let Ben and Colby have a couple of twists so they could be walruses too. We settled down when the lunch monitor headed in our direction.

Finally it was activity period. I'd used my new pink eraser to remove Ben's name from the top of one of his quizzes and added my own. Mrs. Preston gave me a hall pass, and I was on my way to Mr. Potter's room.

Desks were pulled together in pairs, and kids, also mostly in pairs, were hunched over papers and math books at many of them, muttering softly. I spotted Macy with a younger girl and sat at the empty desk closest to them. I made a little noise arranging my chair, and Macy looked up. She smiled and held up a finger to let me know she'd be with me in a minute.

I arranged my supplies—my book, paper, ruler, pencil, and pink eraser—neatly on the desk while I waited for her. When she slipped into the chair beside me, my hands started to sweat.

"You missed the game yesterday," I whispered.

"Dentist appointment," she said softly. I wondered because of the look on her face if she had a toothache. "I heard Noah got hurt. Is he okay?"

"Yeah," I said. "No brain, no pain. He was just mad that the coach wouldn't put him back in."

"Dave says they'd have won if Noah hadn't gone out." She had a little smile on her face that showed me how special she thought her brother was. "Well, you're not here to talk about soccer. What do you need help with?"

I showed her my paper. I mean Ben's.

"I guess we better go back to the basics," she said, with a little shake of her head.

"I'm so confused," I told her. And that was the truth. I had no idea how Ben had come up with the answers he'd written down.

By the end of activity period, I was adding and subtracting fractions with no trouble at all.

"We've made a lot of progress!" Macy exclaimed, thrilling me with her eye-scrunching smile.

"You're a good teacher," I told her as I put my supplies back in my backpack.

"If you need help again," she said, "I'll be here."

"We won't be meeting every week?"

She laughed. "I'll let you decide that."

I was so excited when I left Mr. Potter's room that I had a hard time not running down the hall.

(12)

Big Brother Is Watching

On Thursday I had a chance to write Grandpa's snowstorm story in my journal. I added what he'd said about everyone feeling small in a blizzard. I was glad I had that to think about when we were getting organized for our classroom picture for the yearbook. I tried to stand on the back row of the risers beside Ben. The photographer began to re-arrange people. I sunk a little lower, hoping he wouldn't even notice me. But he was paid to notice all of us, and to make us smile so our parents would be proud. "There's a little guy in the back row that I can't see," he said. I stood on my tiptoes. "Yes, you, in the Yankees T-shirt. I'm going to need you to move down a row so I can see your face. Switch places with that tall girl in front of you." Shannon and I wiggled past each other, taking our new positions. "No. That's still not going to work." This photographer was taking his job way too seriously. He stepped over to our class and turned kids a little to the side here and a little to the side there, making a space for me right up front. I might change grades every year, and school buildings every few years, but I would always be in the front row of classroom photos. The only boy in a line of girls.

When Ben and I were walking home that day, I heard someone gaining on us. I turned to see Wes Powers a few feet away. A moment later he was beside me, and then he was standing in front of me on the sidewalk. I had to stop walking or I'd have run right into him.

"Stay away from her," he said, poking a finger at my face.

I took a step backward. "What are you talking about?"

Wes stepped closer and leaned toward my face. "You know exactly what and who I mean. She used to talk to me. Until you started coming to the school store. And talking to her at soccer games. And going for tutoring." Wes's eyes got narrower and narrower as he talked.

"He really needs that math help," Ben volunteered.

Wes pointed at Ben. "You stay out of it."

"Just stay cool, man," Ben said, raising his arms. But Wes was looking at me.

"I'm just a little sixth-grader," I said, my voice squeaking. "Why would she like me?"

Wes grinned. "I'm glad you know your place, shrimp. Just stay away."

Wes pushed past some other kids who'd caught up to us and crossed the street. My heart was pounding like a soccer ball slamming into a practice target.

"What a creep!" Ben said. "He can't do that to you. Let's go after him."

I tried to swallow the dryness out of my throat. "No. He's right, you know. I am just a shrimpy sixth-grader. She can't really like me."

"But she does," Ben said. "I've seen it with my own eyes. Your size doesn't matter to her."

"It matters to *me!*" I yelled at him. "I acted small, and I am small. Let's just stay out of his way."

"But—" Ben tried.

"I don't want to talk about it!"

I tried to work on my homework at the fitness center, but I kept thinking about Wes Powers, and my heart would pound again. Mom thought I looked flushed and let me buy a soda from the store next door.

We waited until Noah returned home from his away game to have supper. He was excited about the Titans' victory over a tough opponent and told us how Dave, once again, hadn't let anything slip past him. I wondered if Dave had anyone there to cheer him on. I'd have asked Noah, but sometimes people can read between the lines when you don't want them to.

I couldn't think of anything I needed at the school store Friday morning. Maybe if Macy started working a different day of the week, I'd go back in and look around, but I doubted it.

Because I hadn't finished my homework or studied at all, I didn't do very well on my spelling test and barely passed my math quiz. I thought it was kind of funny that I had a paper of my own to take to tutoring now that I wasn't going again, but I forgot to laugh.

Noah had made plans to go to O'Rourke's Saturday but was home Friday night, so Mom and Dad went out on a date. They ordered pizza for Noah, Emma, and me before they left and told us to behave ourselves.

"Can we eat in the TV room?" Emma asked after they'd gone.

"I don't care," Noah said. "But we're not watching Animal Planet. They have vet shows on this time of day."

So we set up the TV trays and watched cartoons while we ate.

When the phone rang, Emma ran to answer it. "No, they're not here right now. I think they're in China."

Noah laughed. "Is she being funny on purpose, or does she really think the Chinese restaurant is in China?"

"It's hard to tell with Emma," I said.

After she hung up, Noah went to his room to make a phone call.

"I know what we can do," Emma said to me.

"What makes you think I want to do anything but watch cartoons?" I muttered.

"Because Mom's not here, and we can slide down the laundry chute!"

"That was a stupid idea, Emma." I didn't budge from the couch or even look at her.

Emma pulled on my arm. "No, it wasn't. It will be fun. C'mon, before we get too big. This may be our last chance."

"Yeah, right," I said. "I'm going to wake up "Big" some morning, just like Tom Hanks."

"You're no fun." Emma dropped my arm.

I looked at her and felt bad about being so grouchy. "All right. But I'm just sliding down. I'm not going to pretend we're at the fair, or we're escaping from an airplane, or anything."

"I'll fix a soft landing!" Emma said and ran into the bathroom to pile up laundry at the bottom of the chute.

I slid first and waited downstairs for Emma. It didn't feel as exciting as it had when I was younger, but we kept hiking upstairs and sliding down. Until Mom and Dad came home.

I climbed out of the chute, and there was Mom standing in the bathroom, hands on her hips. "Michael. You've got to stop doing that. You could break a leg or, worse yet, get stuck in there. How do you think we'd get you out? I'm not tearing apart my bathroom walls."

"Sorry, Mom," I said as Emma tumbled out of the chute.

"It's not dangerous, Mom. Really. You should try it," Emma coaxed. But Mom, not amused, ushered us out of the bathroom.

I decided to find something to do in my room. Noah's door was open, and he noticed me passing by. "Why the long face?" he said.

"I like this girl at school," I blurted out. "But somebody else likes her too."

Noah put his feet up on his computer desk and motioned for me to sit on his bed. "Who does the girl like?" he asked.

"Me, I think. At least I know she doesn't like him."

Noah grinned. "So what's the problem?"

I shrugged my shoulders and then admitted it. "He told me to stay away from her."

Noah laughed. "You're going to listen to him?"

"He's older. And about a foot taller than me, Noah!"

My brother started to look mad. "Who is he? I'll take care of him."

"You can't do that. I have to do this by myself. I just don't know how."

Noah wheeled his chair toward the bed and leaned close to me. "You'll need to find his weak spot, Mike. Everybody has one, even bullies. *Especially* bullies."

"All I know is, he's a creep."

Noah laughed again. "You'll have to outsmart him. Make him look like a fool."

"That's easy for you to say, when you can back it up with size."

"It'll work out, Mike." He slapped me on the shoulder. "And I'll help whenever you say the word."

"Thanks." I stood up to leave.

Noah spun back to his computer, then looked at me again. "Hey, who's the girl?"

"I'd rather not say yet. I'll tell you if it all works out."

Noah nodded. "Gook luck. You gotta go for it, you know. Stand tall, man."

Yeah, I thought, great advice for a kid who can still fit in the laundry chute.

(13)

Bigger Is Better

The best thing about the whole next week was that Mrs. Preston had loved Grandpa's tall tale. But at the end, where I'd written what he said about a big storm making everyone feel small, she wrote this question, "When have you felt big?"

What a joke, I thought. Maybe I could tell her about the first day of school, when somebody thought I was in the wrong building. Or how big I'd felt with Wes leaning over me. How about the time I'd gotten mad at a soccer player and his teammate said to him, "Be careful that Shorty here doesn't bite you in the kneecap"? And had she forgotten the soccer-jersey "dress" story? "Stand tall," Noah had said. That was a joke too.

I told Mom I was going to Ben's house Tuesday after school.

"You *can* come over," Ben said as we walked, "but I think we should go to Noah's game."

"Go if you want. I'm sick of soccer. I have other friends I can hang out with, you know." I kicked a stone out of my way, and it clattered against a garbage can sitting on the curb.

Ben shook his head. "I wish you'd quit feeling sorry for yourself."

"Why should I? Nothing is ever going to change. I'm a runt. I'm going to be small forever!"

"Yeah . . . but I never saw you *act* it before."

"Get used to it. What you see is what you get." I started to walk faster to get away from him, but Ben started walking faster too, and stayed right beside me.

We rode our skateboards in Ben's driveway till Mom picked me up after the game. Another winner for Dave and the boys. If they kept this up, the Titans would be in the championship game at the end of the season. Too bad I wouldn't be able to make it to any more of the games.

I didn't go to Mr. Potter's room for math help on

Wednesday. It seemed a lot more important to write in my journal. I dated the top of the page and wrote, "When have I felt big?" beneath it. Then I sat and wondered what to write next. I'd have to make something up because "Never!" wouldn't fill up the whole page. Unless I wrote it a million times.

Finally I crossed out the question, skipped a line, and wrote what was on my mind.

I don't think I like the idea of having to write in this journal all year long. I know you said it's a good way to record what happens in sixth grade. But maybe not everyone wants to remember what sixth grade was like. Maybe sixth grade is a year some people will want to forget, but they won't be able to because of these journals. Maybe kids who get 100 all the time will want to remember. Maybe spoiled rich kids like to remember all the stuff they get. Maybe pretty girls or tough guys want to remember how popular they are. Probably the president of student council will be happy to have that written down. But average kids and below-average kids may not think this is such a special year to remember. And I thought that journals were supposed to be private, but you read ours every

week. I'll write one page because I have to, but
don't expect me to go over that ever again.

I had to write that last sentence in tiny letters to
keep it from going onto the next page. The only
thing I felt good about when I finished writing was
that I didn't have to do any more of it that week.

I also didn't have to think up a plan to avoid the
next soccer game because it was away again, and it's
too hard for Mom and Dad to leave work early
enough to make it to those games.

My grumpy attitude at school was showing up at
home too. Emma was avoiding me, and Mom wondered if she should make an appointment with Dr.
Seltzer for me to have a checkup.

When Noah announced that he'd be going to
O'Rourke's on Friday, Mom said, "You are always
going over there. Why doesn't Dave come here
sometime?"

Noah got busy pulling his dirty soccer uniform
out of his gym bag. "Uh, I'll ask him." Then Noah
went to his room to do his homework and check his
e-mail.

I made sure my homework was done too. I wasn't
about to make the same mistake two weeks in a row.

Then I watched TV. They kept showing the same fast-food commercial over and over again. Everybody in the commercial was so happy because they could supersize their value meals. What is with that? How come everybody wants things bigger all the time? Why aren't *regular* and *large* good enough for people? Where does *small* fit in a supersized world?

"Bigger isn't always better," I muttered at the TV, but I'd never heard of people wanting to *minisize* anything. I'm pretty sure those commercial people laughed at me while they stuffed their faces. Maybe it was gas from all the overeating.

(14)

It's Not the Size That Matters

I never expect more than the one page that I've asked for, legibly written, by the end of the week. Certainly, what you write about is up to you. Michael, is there something going on that you would like to talk, rather than write, to me about?

That's what Mrs. Preston had written in her thin, swirly cursive in my journal.

I didn't want to talk to her. I didn't want to write to her either, but she'd made it plain that I couldn't get out of that. I caught her watching me several times over the next couple days. She always smiled, and I smiled back, wanting to show her that I was okay, even though nothing had changed and never would.

When the kids who play in band went to rehearsal Wednesday afternoon, Ben left the room too. I thought he must have gone to the boys' room, but he didn't come back until the end of activity period, just in time to pack up for home.

I shouldered my backpack as we exited the building and checked to make sure Wes wasn't hanging around. "I thought we were going to work on our science project, Ben. Where were you?"

"In Mr. Potter's room." He said it like it was no big deal!

My mouth dropped open, and I stared at him for a moment before speaking. "You went for math help?"

Now Ben looked around. "Shh! Someone might hear you. I didn't exactly go for help. I only went because you wouldn't."

I didn't want to be interested, but I couldn't help myself. "Was she there?"

"Uh-huh." Ben grinned.

"And?"

"I think she misses you. She asked me why you

hadn't come back for more help. And why you weren't at the soccer game. She asked me questions about your family too."

"Like what?" My hands were getting sweaty.

"Like if I'd ever been to your house, and if your parents are as nice as they seem."

"Why would she ask that?"

Ben shrugged. "I don't know. Maybe she's trying to work up the nerve to come over."

"That's got to be it! Now what do I do?"

"You've got to work up your nerve too. You've got to stop running scared."

"But running is one of my best things. Noah told me to stand tall, but I'm much better at running." I could feel my sense of humor returning. "Why do you think it was easier to stand up to the roller-coaster man than a pimple-faced eighth-grader?" I wondered out loud.

"Beats me," Ben said.

"That's probably it. The roller-coaster man might have hollered at me, but Wes could try to beat me up. He wouldn't have to try very hard to succeed, either."

"I guess if Wes bothers you again, you could always start running. I doubt he's as fast as you."

"Yeah," I said, standing as tall as I possibly could, "I'm sure I could outrun him."

The next day, at the top of the next clean page in my notebook journal, I wrote the question "When have I felt big?" one more time. Then I wrote all about standing up to the roller-coaster man. I didn't care that I had to use almost two whole pages to say what I wanted. And even though I didn't write it down, I'd decided to stand up to Wes too.

(15)

High Fives

My whole family was able to go to Noah's soccer game on Saturday. Macy's whole family was there too. Even though they always sit in the bleachers, they spent some time before the game talking to us on the sidelines.

"I've been wanting to meet you and thank you for putting up with Noah so often," Mom said.

"He's a nice young man. We're happy to have him." Mrs. O'Rourke smiled, which made her look a lot like Macy.

"That's always good to hear, but I want you to know that the kids are welcome to be at our house too. Though I think Noah enjoys time away from his younger siblings."

"That's me!" Emma announced. All the adults laughed.

"Mom," Macy said, putting her hand on my arm, "this is Michael."

"Well, hello. Macy's told me all about you. You're every bit as cute as she said you were."

I wanted to crawl in a hole. I couldn't remember a time I'd ever felt more embarrassed. Then Mrs. O'Rourke said, "How are things going with math now, Michael?"

"Fine," I croaked. Mom and Dad had confused looks on their faces, and I hoped they'd forget about this by the time we were alone. I wondered exactly how much Macy had told her mother. Stand tall, stand tall, stand tall, I kept telling myself as Dad and Mr. O'Rourke started talking about the upcoming championship game.

Macy bent close to whisper in my ear. My arm still felt tingly where she'd touched it, and now this. "I'm sorry Mom mentioned the tutoring. I hope you're not embarrassed. I hope it won't keep you from coming back."

I tried to sound more grown-up than I felt. "Sure. Not a problem."

"Well, we better grab some seats," Mrs. O'Rourke said to her husband, then turned back to Mom. "We should all get together for a family dinner sometime."

"That would be lovely," Mom said.

"Want to sit with us?" Macy asked me.

"No, thanks," I said, my courage failing completely in front of our families. "I like to stay close to the action."

"I'll sit with you!" Emma said, and she bounced off to where I didn't dare go.

I was glad it was time for the game to begin. The close score and tough competition kept it an exciting game to watch, but every now and then I'd sneak a look into the bleachers and see Macy and Emma laughing. I wondered if they were talking about me. Next time Macy asked, if she ever did again, I would sit with them.

The Titans were victorious again. After all the hugging, cheering, and high fives, Mom insisted that we go out for lunch to celebrate, even though

Noah said he needed to shower so he could go to O'Rourke's.

"You haven't been hanging out with any of your other friends now that you're friends with Dave," I said to him in the minivan on the way to the diner. It seemed pretty unfair that *he* was spending all this time at Macy's house.

"You should talk," he said. "Look at you and Ben."

"At least Ben comes over to our house as much as I go there."

"Maybe that's because neither you nor Ben have pesky little brothers." Noah squirted me with his water bottle.

I used my shirt to dry my face. "We have pesky Emma, though, and that doesn't stop him from coming over!"

"*Mom,*" pesky Emma whined.

"Michael!" Mom warned from the front seat.

"Why am I in trouble? Noah started it!"

Noah squirted me with his bottle again, and I squawked.

"That's enough, Michael," Dad said, also from the front.

"But—"

"I said, that's enough."

"Sorry," I mumbled, water dripping from my face onto my wet shirt.

Noah and Emma reached over my head to give each other another high five.

(16)

Growing Up

Mrs. Preston loved my story about the roller coaster. She wrote, "Good for you! We all grow a bit when we stand up for ourselves. However, I must caution you to use good sense and treat people with respect."

I didn't let what she said about using good sense keep me from going to tutoring on Wednesday.

"Phew," Ben said when he learned I was going. "I don't think I could have taken that kind of pressure again." He slapped me on the back. "Good to have you back to normal." He handed me his latest quiz. I was sure Macy could help me in no time at all.

She grinned when she saw me. "I'm glad you came back. My mom can say embarrassing things sometimes."

"Parents are like that," I agreed. "But mine are nice. You should come over sometime, and you'd see." I couldn't believe I'd said it. My whole face felt like it was on fire. I wiped my damp hands on my jeans.

Macy giggled and blushed a little herself. Then she nodded. "I just might do that." Then she changed the subject, which was a good thing because Mr. Potter was moving around the room and stopping at each pair of desks to see how the tutors and pupils were doing. By the end of activity period I knew how to do every problem on Ben's paper perfectly.

I couldn't wipe the grin off my face for the rest of the day.

"You're not worried about Wes anymore?" Ben asked me on the way home.

I laughed recklessly. "I have my running shoes on." I planned to wear them for the rest of my life.

Or at least until Wes graduated and moved on to wherever it is that bullies go after high school.

I don't know how Wes came by his information, but by the next afternoon he knew that I'd seen Macy again. This time I heard leaves crunching beneath his feet as he came up behind us.

"I thought I told you to stay away from her!" he growled in my ear.

"I'm afraid I can't do that," I said. "She likes me."

"She's got good taste, don't you think?" Ben said.

Wes leaned close to Ben. "Are you making fun of me?"

Ben backed up a step. "No, not at all."

It must have been the combination of nerves and excitement that made me giggle a little bit just then.

Wes was in my face in a flash. "Do you think this is funny? I could beat you up, you little punk."

"I'm sure you could," I said, "but you'd have to catch me first."

I took off on a dead run then, scattering leaves as I flew down the sidewalk.

"Hey! Get back here, peewee!" Wes yelled from

behind me. But I wasn't stupid enough to turn around and go back.

By the time I got to the ball flats, my heart was pounding so hard, it felt like raging floodwaters inside my chest. I spotted one of the DPW's drainage pipes lying on a little slope and crawled inside so I could rest. The cool pipe felt good against my face.

After my breathing slowed down a bit, I peeked out. I saw some walkers in the distance, but none of them were Wes. I began to feel worried about Ben. Had Wes done something to *him* because I'd run away? I wished we had come up with a plan of some kind.

When the coast was clear, I slid out of the pipe and headed back toward where I'd abandoned Ben. I didn't get very far before I spotted him with Colby and Philip. When we met up, they cheered and gave me high fives.

"Way to leave Wes in the dust," Philip said.

"What did he do?" I asked.

"He ran after you for about twenty yards, then gave up," Ben said. "By then these guys had caught up to me, so I started walking with them. Wes swore at us as we walked by him, then he went off in another direction. Probably to crawl back in whatever hole he came from."

"Ben told us that Wes is out to get you," Colby said. "We'll watch your back."

"What does he have against you, anyway?" Philip asked.

I was glad Ben hadn't told them. "Uh, he thinks I took something that belonged to him." I laughed. "What an imagination."

We'd reached the fitness center, so I said good-bye and went in.

Later that night, after I'd gone to bed, Noah came into my room. "I heard you're having some trouble at school."

I sat up in bed. "What are you talking about?"

"Your math."

I shrugged. "Oh, yeah. A little. It's no big deal."

"Maybe I can help," he offered.

"I've got it covered, but thanks."

Noah nodded. "How are things going with that girl?"

"Great," I said. "I took your advice, and I think I'm winning. She might even come over soon."

Noah saluted me. "Well done. 'Night, man."

"'Night, Noah. Thanks."

As he started to close my door I called out to him. "Don't say anything to Mom and Dad, okay? About the math or the girl."

"Gotcha."

(17)

You Had Me a Little Worried!

We had a long weekend because of Columbus Day. We didn't go away or anything, because Noah had soccer practice on Saturday and Monday.

Tuesday was Noah's last home game of the soccer season. The sun shone brightly, but it was a blanket-and-hot-chocolate kind of day. Mom's folding chairs were full.

The crowd that gathered to watch was bigger than usual because if they won this game, the Titans would be playing in the championship game on Saturday.

Even though I do like to be close to the action on

the field, I sat with Macy during the first half of the game. It wasn't like a real date or anything because Macy's mom was on the other side of her, and Emma was on the other side of me. But as we sat there talking, I was sure I'd be able to tell Noah about her soon.

Ben showed up with Homer at halftime. As much as Emma likes Macy, Macy was no competition for that hound dog. After Emma abandoned us, I began to feel a little awkward sitting with the O'Rourkes and joined Ben on the sidelines. Emma had gone off with Homer on his leash.

Tension mounted in the second half when the opposition scored a goal that tied the game. They made several more shots that Dave stopped. With seconds remaining in regulation play, Noah was able to slip through their defense and score the winning goal. The goal that sent them to the championship game!

As soon as the game clock ran out, everybody screamed and hollered and rushed at the players. And everybody hugged everybody—parents and players and friends. Our whole family grabbed Noah in a big family hug. Mom even hugged Dave O'Rourke. Macy hugged Dave *and* Noah. Then Macy hugged Emma.

Then Macy hugged me! Talk about tingly. Homer was even getting in on the action, barking his fool head off. I'd never felt so wonderful in my whole life.

Macy was still excited about Noah's goal when I went for tutoring on Wednesday. "He's a hero," she said.

"What about Dave? If he hadn't stopped those shots, the other team would have won."

"True. But it was still Noah who scored the winning goal." Macy's eyes shone.

Mr. Potter headed in our direction, and I showed Macy all the mistakes on the paper I'd brought with me.

"I don't understand how you can do so well with me on Wednesday and have so much trouble on your Friday quizzes," she said, shaking her head.

"It's a mystery to me too," I said as sadly as possible.

"Maybe you'd do better if someone else helped you instead of me." Macy sounded disappointed, and I was worried.

"I don't think so! I was just distracted last week. I, uh, had a run-in with this other kid, but that's all fixed now, so don't worry about it, and I'm sure if you help me now, I'll do much better on Friday. Please?"

The words came out in a rush. Then I smiled. "I re-member how to add fractions. Want to see?"

Macy laughed, and our tutoring session began.

Too soon I was packing up to leave.

"See you at the championship game," Macy said. "If they win, that will be the best birthday present ever."

"Is Saturday your birthday?" I asked.

Macy nodded and scrunched up her face in that beautiful smile of hers.

I couldn't talk to Ben about this on the way home because there were four of us walking together every day now, and I wasn't ready to tell my bodyguards about Macy. Everyone would know soon enough.

After supper I called Ben. I doodled hearts and flowers with thorny stems while I talked. "So I was thinking that I'd go to the florist by Mom's center af-ter school on Friday and buy a rose for Macy."

"I don't know, Mike. I'm not sure that's such a good idea."

"Why not? Girls love smelly things. A rose would be a perfect birthday present," I insisted.

"Has Noah gone to O'Rourke's this week?"

"Yeah," I said. "He went over for a little game cel-ebration after supper last night."

"Did he go *to* the O'Rourkes' or someplace *with* the O'Rourkes?"

"What difference does it make?" I said. "Why are you changing the subject? I was talking about Macy's birthday."

"I know," he said dully. Was I boring him or something? "I don't think you should get her a rose, okay? Maybe you should back off a bit."

I was getting annoyed. And a little scared. "Has Wes said something to you?"

"No! She's just so much older than you. Bigger too. Isn't there somebody in our grade, someone younger and smaller, that you like better?" Ben was practically whining. "How about the new girl, that little red-head? She seems to like you."

I wasn't doodling anymore. "What has gotten into you? You know Macy likes me too! You've told me so yourself."

"Yes, I have," he muttered. "I'm just trying to be a good friend. Forget it. Forget I said anything. I guess I just don't feel too well."

"Geez, you had me worried for a minute," I said, relaxing a bit. "I thought Wes had rounded up a bunch of thugs to ambush us on the way home or something." I laughed a little.

"No, nothing like that. Well, I better go. I have math homework to do."

After I hung up, I realized Ben must really be sick. He was so sick, he'd forgotten that he didn't *do* homework.

(18)

Cut Down to Size

Ben still didn't act well on Thursday. At lunchtime I told him he should have stayed home from school. "Maybe I will tomorrow," he said.

I tried to cheer him up by breathing on my spoon and hanging it off my nose. It didn't work, but everyone else got a little wild and crazy.

Pretty soon our lunch monitor came over to our table. "You kids need to settle down. Stop trading and playing with your food."

"We're not trading and playing with our food. We're trading and playing with this." I held up the rubbery cafeteria hot dog I'd taken off Colby's lunch tray and shook it.

I could tell by the twitching at the corners of her mouth that our lunch monitor was working very hard not to laugh. "All right, then," she finally said, shaking her fistful of straws at us, "just settle down."

Everybody laughed.

"That was close," Colby said.

After lunch I wrote in my journal all about Tuesday's exciting game and the upcoming championship game on Saturday. I told Mrs. Preston how proud of Noah I was and how I wanted to play just like him when I got older. I reminded her that I would be a Titan, playing on the high-school team in a few years. I could hardly wait!

I saw Wes hanging around the playground when we left school on Thursday, but I felt completely safe with all my buddies around.

Grandma called Thursday night to say that she and Grandpa would come up for the weekend to watch Noah's game and say good-bye before heading for Florida. Their *Old Farmer's Almanac* was predicting an early winter, and like Grandpa had already told me, he wanted to be down south before any snow fell.

When I told Mom on Friday morning that I didn't think Ben would be going to school, she said she'd take me on her way to work. That meant Emma and Kimmy would be riding also. Then Ben showed up at the last minute. "I'll drive you anyway," Mom said when she looked at him.

After she dropped us off, Ben said, "I'm not sick. I need to talk to you, Mike."

"Is there a problem at your house?" I asked. That didn't seem likely, but this wasn't like Ben.

"No. Just come over after school." Ben was not looking at me.

"Okay," I said, "but we'll have to stop and tell Mom. And you'll have to go with me to buy the rose! And also, I'll have to be home for supper. Gram and Gramp are coming. Can I leave the rose at your house and pick it up tomorrow?"

Ben shook his head. "Whatever."

"Thanks. Boy, is this going to be the best weekend ever!"

What are the chances that Colby and Philip would both be absent on the same day? But they were. When leftover hot dogs showed up as a lunch choice, I put two and two together. "Don't eat them," I told everyone. "They probably made Colby and Philip sick!"

Even Ben laughed. He must be feeling a lot better to know he would soon be getting his problem off his chest, I thought.

Without the extra muscle around for our walk home, Ben and I decided to take our time leaving. We thought that if we waited a few extra minutes, Wes would leave ahead of us, and we wouldn't have to worry about him. We also decided to go out the side door rather than the front so we could see if he was hanging around the playground before he could see us.

Wrong. And wrong again!

As soon as we set foot outdoors Wes's big hands pinned me to the brick wall. Another goon grabbed hold of Ben.

"You can't run this time, pip-squeak. Why am I having to tell you *again* to stay away from her?"

I gulped. "Because I didn't listen the first two times?" I said.

Wes grinned and messed up my hair with his sweaty hand.

"Hey," Ben hollered. "Leave him alone."

"Why should I? He's got a hearing problem," Wes yelled in my face. "Maybe I should clean out your ears. How would that be, Shorty?"

"It's not Mike that she likes," Ben shouted. "It's his older, *much* bigger brother, Noah. From the *high* school."

Wes and I both stared at him. I felt the energy go out of Wes like air going out of a balloon.

"What did you say?" I wasn't sure I'd heard Ben right. Maybe I *did* need my ears cleaned out.

"You're a liar," Wes said.

Ben shook the other boy's hands off his arms. "It's true. I saw them holding hands Tuesday night at the ice-cream shop."

The four of us stood there for a moment, trying to make sense of what Ben was saying. I felt like I'd been punched in the gut. . . . By Ben instead of Wes. Wes looked the same way. Just for a moment. Then he looked like a creep again. He pointed his fingers at us. "Losers." Then he and his punk friend walked away.

I turned on Ben. "I thought you were my friend!"

Ben looked droopy, like the air had been let out of him too. "I had to do it. You had to know."

"Like that? In front of Wes?" I glared at him.

Ben shook his head. "I didn't *want* to do it then.

I didn't want to do it at all. That's what I was going to tell you at my house."

"I was going to buy her a stinking rose," I said, kicking at the leaves with my feet. "Were you going to let me do that?"

"I was going to tell you at my house," he repeated.

"I feel like an idiot," I said. "How could they do this to me? How could she say all those things about liking me?"

"She *does* like you, Mike. The way a girl likes her boyfriend's kid brother. Think about it. She wasn't trying to trick you. She was being honest. We just took it the wrong way."

We were near Fit and Trim. Emma and Kimmy were going in. "Tell Mom I'm going to Ben's house," I called to Emma.

"What will you give me?" she asked.

"Just *do* it," I yelled.

"O*kay*, grouchy!" She jutted her chin forward and stuck her nose in the air.

Ben and I took Homer for a walk so we could keep talking privately. I told Ben everything Macy had ever said to me. It all made perfect sense now. The way Noah had been acting about going over to O'Rourke's and everything.

"He never said he was going to *Dave's* house," I recalled. "He always said *O'Rourke's*. That was sneaky."

"Remember when Macy said that she came to soccer games to see *other* people?" Ben dragged Homer away from a garbage can.

"Yeah. She didn't mean me, like we thought she did. It's been Noah the whole time." I fingered the money in my pocket. The money that I'd planned to spend on a rose.

"That should make you feel a little better," Ben said.

"How do you figure that?" I asked. We had come to a complete stop so Homer could sniff a lamppost.

"Well, she didn't start out liking you and then dump you for your brother."

I nodded. "Still, this is definitely not a year I'm going to want to remember."

(19)

A Little Under the Weather

I wasn't in a very good mood for Grandma and Grandpa's visit. I didn't act mean or anything, just kind of quiet. When I didn't eat much of my dinner at the restaurant Friday night, Mom wondered if I had caught something from Ben. I told her she was probably right. I figured if everyone thought I was a little sick, they wouldn't nag me with questions about what was wrong with me. But I'd have to find a way to snap out of it before Mom decided to take me to Dr. Seltzer. I figured I had about three days. I didn't have any experience with this sort of thing, but three days didn't seem like enough time to get over a broken heart.

Grandma said, "I've got just the thing to put a smile on his face once we're back at the house. You too, Emma. I've made Halloween costumes for you!"

"Yippee!" Emma said. "What did you make?"

"That's a secret," Grandma whispered.

"My little bundle," Grandpa said gently, "Michael here probably wasn't planning to go trick-or-treating this year. Were you, boy?"

Actually, Ben and the bodyguards and I had been planning to dress up as gangsters and roam around town for a while. We figured you're never too old for a little free candy. But Grandpa obviously thought I *was* too old. If I said I was going, he might think I was a baby. If I said I wasn't, it would hurt Grandma's feelings. And she'd made me a costume. Mom knew I was in a tricky spot. I could see her holding her breath, waiting for my answer.

"Actually," I said, "I wouldn't mind dressing up to take Emma and her friends around." I could tell by everyone's faces that it was a good answer. Mom started to breathe again. Emma didn't even seem in-sulted. A spelling word we'd had recently came to my mind: *diplomacy*. I was sure Mom would let me off the hook to go with the guys when Halloween arrived.

Back at the house, Grandma handed the paper bags with the costumes to Emma and me. "Go put them on and give us a fashion show," she said.

Emma skipped up the stairs two at a time. I walked a bit more slowly, which is excusable if you don't feel too well. I wondered what the chances were that I'd find a gangster costume inside. Probably slim, since I hadn't let anyone know my plans.

I closed my bedroom door and dumped the costume on my bed. What was this? Riding pants? A silky jacket and cap? Boots? A racing whip?

I am not a boy who swears, but if I were, I would have let loose a whole string of cusswords. Grandma had made me a jockey outfit. I hoped it wouldn't fit.

A few minutes later, I heard a knock on my door. "Michael," Mom called, "do you need any help?"

"Are you alone?" I asked her through the door.

"Yes."

"You can come in, then, but don't laugh."

Mom opened the door. Her hand flew to her mouth when she saw me in the outfit, but not before a giggle burst from her lips. "All you need is a horse," she said from behind her hand.

"Very funny. Maybe I'll go rustle one up."

"That's cowboy talk, Michael. I don't think a jockey would use that language." Mom had put her hand down but was biting her upper lip.

"Do I have to go down there?" I asked.

"I think you do. But don't worry, no one will laugh."

"That's very reassuring to know, since you're standing here splitting a gut!"

"I'm sorry, honey, I'm so sorry." Mom took a deep breath and wiped tears from the corners of her eyes. "Grandma meant well, and she'll want to see you in it. I promise I won't make you wear it for Halloween."

"All right, for Grandma. But I swear, if anyone *grins* the wrong way, I'm not coming out of my room till Christmas!"

"Let me see if Emma needs help, and I'll meet you downstairs." Mom kissed my forehead.

I could tell by the oohs and aahs I heard when I left my room that Emma had beaten me to the living room.

"You'll be so impressed with Michael's outfit too." Mom prepared everyone. "Mother, you shouldn't have gone to so much trouble."

"You know I love to sew," Grandma answered her.

Then Grandma spotted me. She clapped her hands. "How handsome! Just like my brother. Come in, come in, so everyone can see you."

It wasn't until I was standing in the middle of the room that I noticed Macy O'Rourke sitting on the couch between Grandpa and Noah.

I hurried from the room, sure I was going to be sick.

(20)

Life Has Its
Ups and Downs

"**M**ichael, are you okay?" Mom knocked on the bathroom door. "May I come in?"

"No!" I said. "I'll be out in a minute." I soaked a washcloth in cold water, then pressed it against my forehead like Mom always does when I don't feel well. I looked at myself in the bathroom mirror. I had to admit that Grandma was a good costume maker.

Mom was waiting for me outside the bathroom door. "I knew you didn't feel well. Did you throw up?"

"No, but I think I'd like to go to bed now. Would you tell Grandma thanks for making the costume?"

"You can tell her yourself. She'll want to come in and say good night to you." Mom picked up the racing whip and cap and followed me to my room.

"Do you need any help?" Mom asked as she took clean pajamas out of my dresser.

"No." I sat on my bed to take off the boots. "Mom, when did Macy show up?"

"Must be when I came up to check on your costume progress. Do you think she's Noah's girlfriend?"

I shrugged. "I guess. He never told me."

"She's a cutie," Mom said, smiling. "She must have quite a string of admirers."

"I guess," I said again. "Could I be alone now?"

Mom nodded. "I'll bring you some ginger ale in a little while. That's good for tummy trouble." She kissed me again and left my room.

I sat on the edge of my bed a while before putting my pajamas on. I'd been so happy just a few days ago, and look at me now. I remembered an expression I'd heard Mom use before. "Life has its ups and downs." It sure does, I thought. Just like a roller coaster. And sometimes those ups and downs come so close together, you feel sick or a little dizzy, like you've *been* on a roller coaster too.

I looked at Big David swimming around in his bowl on top of my dresser. "You have the perfect life," I said to him. "You don't have to worry about how you fit in. You don't have to worry about bullies, or girls, or where to stand for your class photo. You don't even have to go to school." Ben would have snorted at that one. Man, my David was one big goldfish. "Maybe I should start eating fish food," I told him.

My door opened a crack. "Michael, did you see my costume?"

"Come on in, Emma."

Grandma had made Emma a basset-hound costume.

"Do you like it? Feel the fur." She came over to my bed and stretched her paw toward me.

"Nice," I said. "That's a great outfit for you. Wait till Homer sees you now."

Emma's long ears flapped as she laughed. "Maybe Ben will dress up like a horse and come trick-or-treating with us."

"Naw, that's okay."

"Mom said I have to leave you alone. I have to leave Noah and Macy alone too." Emma scowled.

"It's a good thing Grandma and Grandpa are here. Do you want me to bring you something?"

"I'd take some ginger ale now," I said, leaning back against my pillows.

"I'll bring it right up. Maybe Noah and Macy would like some too. I'm so excited that she's here. Don't you just love her?" I swear Emma's tail wagged.

"Yeah, she's great."

"Do you think Almond Joy is a good name for a hound dog?"

"Perfect," I said, smiling a little as I closed my eyes.

When I heard another tap on my door a couple minutes later, I thought it was Emma returning with my soda.

It was Grandpa, carrying two glasses. He handed one to me. "'Spose ginger ale got its name because it's good for what *ails* you?"

I chuckled.

Grandpa pulled my desk chair close to the bed and sat down. "I know what's the matter with you," he said.

"You do?" I sat up straighter.

"You don't want to be a jockey for Halloween,

but you don't want to hurt your grandma's feelings. Is that it?"

"How did you know?" I asked, relieved that he'd only guessed part of the problem.

"We're a lot alike, Mike. In ways that are much more important than how big we are."

"I don't have anything against jockeys," I said. "They are great athletes. But I'm . . . I'm afraid of horses." Grandpa nodded his head in agreement, so I continued. "And feeling too small already, then dressing as a jockey for Halloween, would be like dressing up as . . . as . . ."

"One of the Seven Dwarfs? A munchkin?" Gramp filled in.

"Yeah, or like Stuart Little," I said.

Grandpa nodded.

"Or like Mini-Me!" I added.

"Who?" Grandpa asked.

"This guy in movies. Never mind. I just want to pretend I'm something *big* when I have a chance. But thanks for understanding."

"Would you like something to go with that soda?"

I shook my head. "You won't tell Grandma, will you?"

"I wouldn't dream of it." He clinked his glass

against mine, like shaking hands on a deal we'd made. "Now tell me what you know about Noah's girlfriend." Grandpa's eyes twinkled.

"She's nice," I said. And I wondered exactly how much else Grandpa had really figured out.

(21)

Big Winners and Big Losers

Grandma volunteered to stay home with me while everyone else went to Noah's game, but I insisted that I felt well enough to go. I didn't really want to see Macy, but I couldn't miss the game.

We hadn't been there very long when Macy found me on the sidelines.

"I was afraid you wouldn't be here," she said to me. "Are you better now?"

I forced myself to smile. "Sure. Happy birthday."

"Thanks!" Macy's eyes disappeared inside her smile. "And thank you for encouraging me to come over to your house. Noah's been inviting me, but you convinced me that it would be okay. Had you figured it out?"

"Had I figured what out?"

"About Noah and me. 'Cause I wanted to tell you, but I had a feeling you put two and two together."

"I'm not that good at math, remember?"

I hadn't meant it as a joke, but Macy thought it was so funny that I ended up laughing too.

"When I saw your Halloween costumes last night, I had this really great idea. What if Noah and I took you and Emma trick-or-treating?"

I wondered when I was going to wake up from this Halloween nightmare. I didn't know what to say.

"If you have other plans," she said, "that's okay."

"I'm just not sure I'm going out this year. I'm getting a little old for that."

"You're kidding! Trick-or-treating is the best. I always dress up."

I didn't have to think of anything to say to that because Grandma had spotted Macy with me and came over to give her a big hug, like she was already a member of the family or something. I wondered if I was going to misunderstand Macy and say foolish things to her for the rest of my life.

The game was about to start. Macy returned to the stands. Grandma tried to get me to sit with her in the lawn chairs, but I needed to pace.

The opposing team took an early lead. Two balls sailed into our goal within the first ten minutes of the game. It looked bad. As if the guys had forgotten how to play as a team, had forgotten that this was an important game, maybe the most important one of their lives. But after that second goal Dave came to life and caught or deflected everything else that came at him. He couldn't win the game all by himself, though.

About five minutes from halftime the mighty, mighty Titans pulled it together. Something clicked, and they began to put plays together. Then they scored, and we went to halftime only one behind.

The pep talk from the coach between halves really fired up the boys. They played their old game throughout the second half, tying things up just moments in. Mom went berserk when Noah scored the third goal. I looked into the stands and saw Macy jumping up and down. Everybody was going crazy, chanting and stomping their feet and blowing horns.

Our fourth goal seemed to clinch it. The opponents couldn't put together another successful play, and the game ended with the Titans victorious. You'd have thought this was a major sports event by all the noise. There was also lots of hugging and high-fiving again, like after the last game. Only I got out of the way before the birthday girl came around.

Later that evening the players had a party to celebrate being regional champions. Grandma and Grandpa said their good-byes the next day. They'd be in Florida till spring.

Now that the excitement of the soccer season was over, our family settled into a new routine that revolved around Noah's basketball practices. He still went to the O'Rourkes' quite often, but Macy was a regular at our house now too. My whole family loved her. I could picture us all going to his basketball games together when they began in late November.

I didn't waste Macy's time tutoring me anymore. I explained to her that something had clicked the last time I'd gone, and everything made sense now. And I meant everything.

I was quite well stocked up on school supplies too. I didn't figure I'd be needing anything from the school store for months. Macy told me that Wes had quit working there. She didn't know why he had, but she was really glad about it.

I was glad to have Wes off my back. I almost felt sorry for him because I understood what he wanted and could never have. I was actually luckier than him because I, at least, had Macy for a friend. He seemed to be avoiding me now too, so he must have been pretty embarrassed.

One night after Macy had gone home, Noah came into my room and asked how things had turned out with that girl I liked.

"She picked an older guy," I said.

"The creep?"

"No. A really nice guy, actually."

Noah shook his head. "Tough. A nice girl will pick you someday. Like Macy. Hang in there."

I wasn't ready to tell him that a certain little redhead named Tina had started to sit with Ben and me during lunch. Or that she and I had exchanged screen names, and that I *might* IM her someday.

Halloween turned out okay. Macy and Noah took Emma and Kimmy all around town. Kimmy actually wore my jockey outfit, and I got to go with the guys. Macy couldn't convince Noah to wear a costume, but she was the most beautiful witch I had ever seen.

Somehow, I found something interesting to write about in my notebook journal every week, and Mrs. Preston kept encouraging me with her comments and questions. Maybe my sixth-grade memories wouldn't be the best ones in my life, but they weren't all bad, and they sure weren't dull.

(22)

Just the Right Size

A couple weeks after Halloween, Ben and I were walking home from school, just the two of us, like old times. The day had started out cool enough, and snow, our first storm of the season, was predicted by morning. The wind picked up in the afternoon as the temperature dropped. The light rain felt like icy jabs against our skin.

Ben pulled his hat down around his ears and stuffed his hands deep in his pockets. "Mom was right. I should have worn gloves today."

"Come on," I said. "We'll stay warmer if we jog."
Ben and I picked up the pace as we cut through the

ball flats. The wind blew my baseball cap off my head, and I ran to catch it. That's when I thought I heard a call for help.

"Did you hear that?" I asked Ben. "It sounds like someone is calling from somewhere." We stopped to listen. At first all I could hear was the rustle of the dead leaves being scattered by the wind. "There. I heard it again. I think it's coming from that DPW pipe."

We hurried to the same drainage pipe I had hidden in a few weeks earlier. "Hello?" I called.

"Help!" A voice called from inside the pipe. "I'm stuck in here."

"Are you hurt?" I asked as I knelt down to peer inside. It was dark in there, but I could see someone partway down the pipe, too far in to reach.

"No, but I'm freezing, and my foot is caught. I don't have any room to get it loose. Man, it's getting cold." The voice sounded a lot like Wes, or what Wes would sound like if he were getting panicky.

"We'll get help," I said.

"Who's in there?" Ben called.

"Wes Powers. Could you hurry!"

Ben and I looked at each other, and I'm sure the same thing was going through his mind that was going through mine. It would serve Wes right if we walked away and left him there.

"You're the runner, Mike. You go, and I'll stay here with Wes."

The rain had changed to a mixture that was mostly snow. I ran as hard as I could to the closest house to the ball flats. It belongs to an old couple who let me use their phone to call 911. Then I ran back to Ben and Wes to wait for the fire department. The old man was behind me. He had a couple of blankets with him and a flashlight, which I used to look up inside the bottom end of the pipe. Wes must have slid down with his leg bent. I could see how his sneaker had his leg wedged against the side of the pipe. He couldn't move his leg up or down.

"Is anybody coming?" Wes whined. "I didn't wear a coat today. I'm really cold."

"A rescue truck is pulling in right now," I said.

"What's going on here?" the first fireman out of the truck asked us. We explained how we'd found Wes.

The fireman looked down the pipe toward Wes's head. "My name is Captain Jones. Are you hurt?"

"No," Wes said, "I just want out of here!"

"Don't worry. We'll get you."

The other fireman looked up the other end of the

pipe like I'd done with the flashlight. "Cap," he said, "we've got to get this kid's sneaker off so he can straighten his leg before we pull him out. No way either of us is going to fit in there. Too bad Morgan's not on duty today."

Captain Jones scratched his head. "We could call him, but it could take quite awhile for him to get here. I don't want Wes in the cold any longer than necessary." The neighbor man had wrapped one of his blankets around Ben and me.

Captain Jones looked at me and smiled. "What's your name, son?"

"Michael Jordan."

"You afraid of small spaces, Michael Jordan?"

"No, sir!"

"You think you can help us out today?"

I stood as tall and straight as I could. "I'm sure I can."

"Here's what we're going to do, then," Captain Jones said, pointing to the other fireman. "Firefighter Marshall is going to fit you with a special helmet so you can see. You are going to slide up the pipe with some surgical scissors, cut Wes's sneaker loose, and pull it off his foot. Then if he can straighten his leg, we'll be able to pull him out from the top side."

"Is there anything we can do?" The old man indicated himself and Ben.

"Call these boys' moms so they're not worried," Captain Jones suggested.

"Use this." Firefighter Marshall handed Ben a cell phone.

I put my baseball cap inside my backpack so it wouldn't blow away, then took the scissors from Captain Jones. I clipped at the air a couple times to see how they worked. Firefighter Marshall put a helmet on my head that had a headlamp attached to the front of it. He adjusted it to fit me.

Marshall looked me in the eyes. "Ready?"

I nodded and took a deep breath. My head felt heavy and wobbly.

I didn't have any trouble shimmying up the pipe to reach Wes. But it was difficult to work the scissors at the right angle to cut his sneaker, especially with cold fingers and my hands up over my head. And hard to cut through that thick material.

"My mom is going to kill me," Wes whined. "These sneakers are brand-new."

Finally I had a big enough slit in the shoe that I was able to work it off his foot. I slid backward out of the pipe with the sneaker in one hand, scissors in the other.

"Good job!" Jones said. "Wes, can you straighten your leg now?"

Wes could, and did. Then he grabbed hold of the rope that the firemen tossed in to him, and Jones and Marshall pulled him out of the pipe. Everybody cheered.

The old man slapped me on the back. Ben gave me a high five. Wes ducked his head and muttered, "Thanks." He didn't seem to want to look at me.

Marshall checked Wes over to make sure he wasn't hurt and wrapped a blanket around him.

That's when I spotted Mom hurrying toward us. She had that same intense expression on her face that she always had at Noah's soccer games.

Ben had explained what was happening when he talked to her on the phone, but I had to go through it all again, adding how Wes had gotten out safely, which she could plainly see.

Captain Jones came over and introduced himself and firefighter Marshall. "We're glad your son was here, Mrs. Jordan. Wes would have been stuck awhile longer if we'd had to wait for firefighter Morgan to get here. He's our little guy on the confined space rescue team, but he's off duty today."

"Your little guy?" I asked. "How little is he?"

"Don't know exactly, but he can't be more than five feet four, five-five at the most. He takes some heavy-duty ribbing about his size at the station, but let me tell you, he's worth his weight in gold when we have to send somebody into a small space. Just like you, Mike. You're our hero today, man." Captain Jones shook my hand.

"Thanks," I said.

Mom beamed at me. "Why was Wes in the pipe?" she asked the captain.

"Seems he was hiding from some high-school boys who have been bothering him."

Ben's and my eyes popped out of our heads. Mom shook hers. "Shame on them! I'll never understand bullies."

"No, ma'am," Jones said, rubbing his hands together. "Well, let's get these boys out of the cold."

He and Marshall shook my hand again. "We'll be in touch," he said.

The firefighters drove Wes home in the rescue truck. We said good-bye to the neighbor man. Mom said she'd drop Ben off at his house on our way home.

"Do you think Noah was one of the high-school kids bothering Wes?" Ben whispered to me as we walked to the car.

"No!" I answered quickly and softly. "He has basketball practice right after school every day. But something tells me Wes's bullying days are over."

Once we were settled in the car, I said, "Did you hear the captain say they have a confined space rescue team, Mom? They're always going to need little guys like me!"

"Michael Jordan, don't you even think about it!"

(23)

News Shorts

We didn't get nearly as much snow that night as what had fallen during the blizzards Grandpa and I talked about, but we did have enough to cancel school the next day.

A reporter came to our house to interview me about what had happened. I felt five feet tall! But this is really funny—the article he wrote about how I'd helped the fire department was in the News Shorts section of the paper. Everybody made jokes about that. This time, I enjoyed them as much as they did.

Mom said, "I *told* you good things come in small packages."

When I called my grandparents to tell them all about it, Gram wondered if that other Jordan boy, the one who plays basketball, would want my autograph now! Gramp said, "Now that you're famous, I hope you won't get too big for your britches."

For days, every time Noah saw me, he'd start to chant, "We are the Titans, the mighty mighty Titans," and give me a high five. Macy gave me a hug and called me a hero. That didn't give me quite as big a thrill as the instant message I got from Tina, which basically said the same thing.

Even pesky Emma told her friends how I'd rescued her once too. I planned to hold that over her head for a long time. Dad said maybe I'd want to trade that jockey costume in for a firefighter's uniform. Mom wasn't excited about that idea.

Like I said, I had a lot to write about in my notebook journal for a while. Stuff I was going to want to remember forever. Like how Captain Jones invited me to the next fire department meeting. He made me a junior firefighter and an honorary member of the confined space rescue team. Then the firefighters gave me a tour of the station. They took me upstairs to their living quarters and opened a hatch in their floor so I could see the pole they slide down. They even demonstrated for me. Now there's a chute I'd like to come down someday! I met firefighter Morgan too. That guy isn't any taller than my grandpa!

Speaking of Grandpa, I can't wait to see what kind of a tall tale he'll tell about this a few years from now.